is Halloween tradition is dedicated in memory of Candice Marie (Allen) Shea.

rowing up, Halloween was a special time of year and one of the most exciting holidays for my mily. We would look forward to the decorations, activities, costumes and of course all of the ndy!

y stepmother's name was Candice, but everyone called her "Candy." Candy would indulge us ery October, as Halloween was one of her favorite holidays. Each year, she would take extra re decorating the house while making treats and goodies for us to enjoy. Candy spent uality time with us creating our costumes and loved trick-or-treating. Her excitement in October as contagious and my Halloween memories as a child are dear to my heart.

ndy passed away in 2011, but her Halloween spirit lives strong in me and my family. My goal ith *The Skeleton in the Closet*® is to share a new Halloween tradition to encourage holiday ctivities between family and friends, in hopes of creating precious memories to cherish for a etime. Enjoy this Halloween by **"playing tricks and giving treats"**™ all season long! Incorpo- te this fun tradition in your family every year and bring Halloween spirit to a whole new level.

om our family to yours, **Happy Halloween and happy trick-or-treating!**

A special thank you to my beautiful wife, business partner and best friend, Jilaine Shea, for your continued support and assitance with all my endevours. I love you, always.

-Chad

Every year, as the weather starts to chill
the Halloween season brings children a thrill.
Witches and goblins, ghouls and ghosts,
but that's not what children focus on most.

They all want to see
how much candy they can eat.
The most important part of Halloween
is a good trick-or-treat!

Each Halloween,
kids fill all of their pockets
with chewys n' goodies
and lollies n' chocolates.

The treats just take over
it's like they can't stop it.
So each and every year
we have a skeleton in the closet.

On the first of October
they'll rise from the dead,
at night, they arrive
while you sleep in your bed.
They'll bring Halloween spirit,
thrills are what they seek.
They'll monitor your spirit
with a good trick-or-treat.

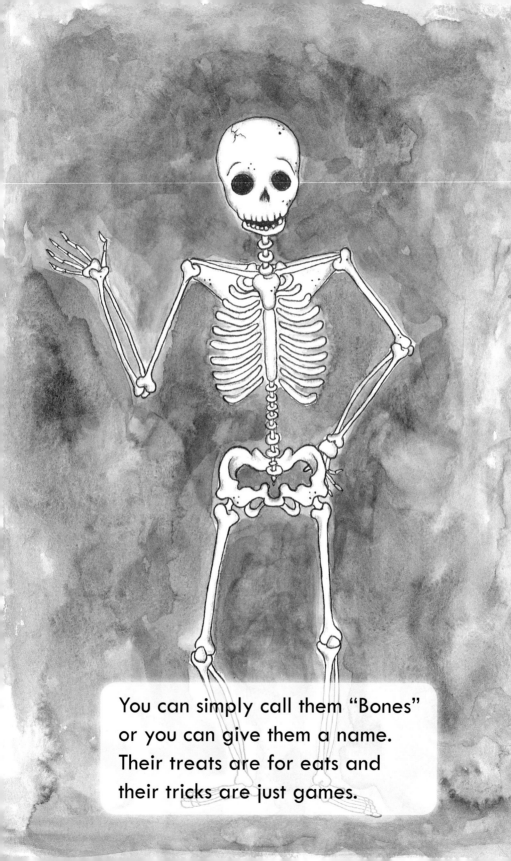

You can simply call them "Bones"
or you can give them a name.
Their treats are for eats and
their tricks are just games.

HALLOWEEN SPIRIT

CERTIFICATE OF AUTHENTICITY.

THIS HALLOWEEN TRADITION BEGAN ON

_____ , 20 _____

THE _____ FAMILY

HAS NAMED THEIR SKELETON

_____

HAPPY TRICK OR TREATING

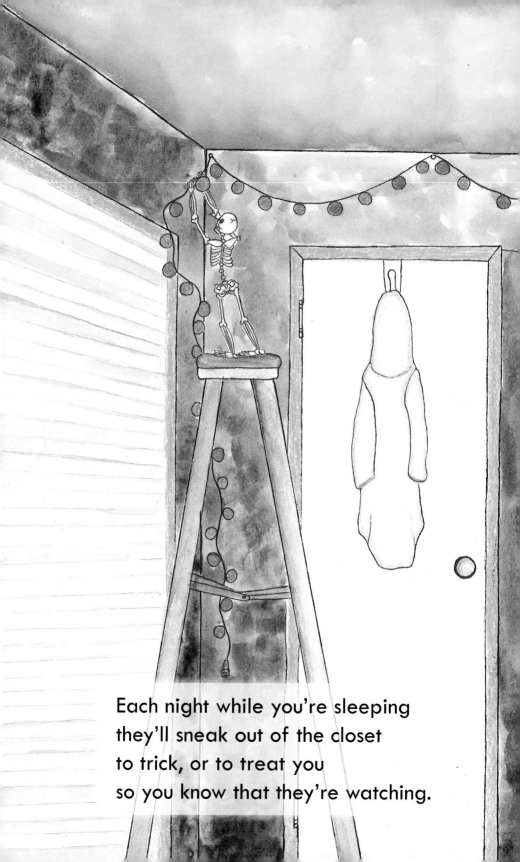

Each night while you're sleeping
they'll sneak out of the closet
to trick, or to treat you
so you know that they're watching.

When they play tricks
it's all just for fun.
Their games are just silly
they can all be undone.

They'll make a mess of your room
or they mix-up your shoes.
They'll drink all your drink
or they eat all your food.

In order to see
the surprise that you've got
you must find them each morning
in a new hiding spot.
The kitchen, the bathroom
or under the bed.
Where would you be
if you were living dead?

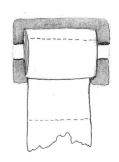

In the first week of October they all want to see decorations on the house... Anything SCARY!

Spiders and cobwebs,
black cats and a mouse,
spooky lights and a coffin...
A proper haunted house.

Once your home
glows orange and black
your skeleton rewards you
with a sweet candy snack.
They'll bring all kinds of candy,
some soft and some hard,
for the second week of October
they want a pumpkin to carve.

A witch on a broom
or a ghost that says "BOO,"
carve a few Jack-O-Lanterns
so the light will shine through.

When the house is decorated
and the pumpkins are carved,
a costume is next
to wear in the dark.

A monster, a mummy,
a hero, a star?
Make sure that it's spooky
whatever you are.

Once you're disguised
from your head to your feet
you're ready to go...
to go "TRICK-OR-TREAT!"

At the end of the evening
on Halloween night,
after all of the fun
and all of the fright,
the skeletons in your closet
will all go away...
Back to the dead,
back to their graves.

Until next Halloween
the graveyard they'll stay.
But they'll haunt you next year
up 'til Halloween day!

About the Author

Chad C. Shea, M.S.B., is the President of Armand Prosper LLC, the publishing company he founded in 2014 working to produce and promote *The Skeleton in the Closet®*. He wrote the charming Halloween tradition in 2013 and it debuted the following year. Chad has an extensive education and background in business, with an emphasis on the entertainment industry. In addition to managing the publishing initiative at Armand Prosper, Chad serves as a media spokesperson for *The Skeleton in the Closet®* and aspires to inspire writers and entrepreneurs alike, worldwide.

Raised in Arizona, Chad is a former Director of Advertising with many years of sales and marketing experience. As an entrepreneur, Shea set his sights in 2014 on producing *The Skeleton in the Closet®* for all to enjoy for years to come. Chad lives with his wife and two children in Orlando, Florida.

About the Illustrator

Danielle Beu is a visionary artist whose creative expression reflects upon the nature of introspection. While transcending worlds of illusion to portray a broader view of awareness, Danielle brings together images of the mystical, miraculous and surrealistic to intertwine with the natural. Working in a variety of mixed mediums (such as watercolors, acrylics, and charcoals as well as her favorite, Crayola Crayons) Danielle has cultivated a variety of whimsical works which reveal her appreciation for the creative processes of all dreaming creatures, in this world and beyond.

Danielle is also an accomplished singer/songwriter and performer with several Disney films & television sound tracks to her credit. As the youngest member of the international, multi-platinum selling pop trio, the "Beu Sisters," she is the recent recipient of the "Artists in Music: Best Pop Artists of 2013 Award."